Seasons at Songbird Cottage (Pleasant Bay Book 5)

Sylvia Price

Penn and Ink Writing, LLC

Stay Up to Date with Sylvia Price

Subscribe to Sylvia's newsletter at newsletter.sylviaprice.com to get to know Sylvia and her family. It's also a great way to stay in the loop about new releases, freebies, promos, and more.

As a thank-you, you will receive a FREE exclusive short story that isn't available for purchase.

Praise for Sylvia Price's Books

"Wow, what a great start to a new series, and I really enjoyed reading it as it was so well-written, and I can't wait to read the next book. This is the first book that I have read by Sylvia Price but not the last and I recommend you read it and you will not be disappointed."

"Author Sylvia Price wrote a storyline that enthralled me. The characters are unique in their own way, which made it more interesting. I highly recommend reading this book. I'll be reading more of Author Sylvia Price's books."

"I love the way this is a very real example of one of the beauties of these small towns! Of course, mixing in beautiful scenery and the growing love with an old friend makes this the perfect start to a new series!"

"I've read several books written by Sylvia Price; she has done a great job at writing a good short story; she is becoming one of my favorite authors. I can't wait to read more of books her books."

"The storyline caught my attention from the very beginning and kept me interested throughout the entire book. I loved the chemistry between the characters."

"The plot flows easily, and the characters are appealing. It's a great story that shows what is most important in life."

"A wonderful, sweet and clean story with strong characters. Now I just need to know what happens next!"

"I just could not put this book down. Thank you for a delightful read."

"I love Sylvia's books because they are filled with love and faith."

"Sylvia's books ooze with love and goodness."

The Christmas Arrival – Available on Amazon

Contents

Chapter One: The Invisible Wedding

"**W**hat do you mean, 'you got married!'" Emma squeaked to her daughter over the phone.

"Exactly that, Mom. Richard and I ran off to Vegas and got married on Tuesday, no, actually, it was Wednesday—Valentine's Day—but we left Nova Scotia on Tuesday. I'm sorry I didn't call to let you know, but we had our reasons, believe me," Claire replied contentedly.

Emma felt as though her balloon had burst. Claire was her firstborn girl, and the daughter most likely to want a picture-book wedding. Emma had kept a place in her heart for the last ten years, where she had dreamed of beautiful white dresses, sumptuous venues, and gloriously decadent reception menus for her eldest daughter. She had given up on her youngest daughter, Izzy, having an archetypal white wedding; even though Isabelle was nearing her thirtieth birthday, she hadn't yet outgrown her penchant for jeans, T-shirts, and playing in a rock band. Claire had been her only shot.

"Why the rush and the secrecy, though? Are you not aware that your dad has budgeted a hundred thousand dollars towards your wedding? All you had to do was wait for his divorce from Linette to be finalized, and you could have had the wedding of your dreams, and not some invisible one."

Claire loved her mother with all her heart. Part of their close bond was the fact that they had never kept secrets from one another. She knew her mom had hoped for a lavish ceremony and a bunch of guests, but she also knew that Emma would never inflict something on her daughters they wouldn't like. She had to get her mother to understand these things.

"I tell you what, Mom, why don't I drive across to Pleasant Bay today? I can tell you everything in full. It's too much to organize my thoughts over the phone. Can you take some stuff out of the freezer for me at Songbird Cottage, please? Just some bread and a couple of chicken breasts. I should get there around lunchtime, but I need to check the ferry schedule first. I'll bring the flash drive with all the wedding pics on it. That'll be faster than emailing them."

"Sure, Claire Bear, that sounds like a good idea. I'll meet you at the cottage. Then we can have a nice chat," Emma said with a more satisfied tone in her voice.

Mother and daughter gave each other an affectionate farewell, and Claire hung up the phone. She turned to her husband, who was lying in bed beside her.

Husband! I can't believe Richard and I are married. It doesn't matter to me how it happened or where the ceremony took place—all I want is to have this wonderful man by my side, forever.

Richard put down the book he was reading. "How did your mother take the news, darling?"

Claire stretched her arms out above her head and arched her back like a cat. "I love Mom so much, but sometimes she makes me laugh. She opts for a quiet little registry office wedding and backyard reception at Songbird Cottage for herself when she married Sam, but she wanted the whole razzle dazzle song and dance for me, bless her heart."

They both chuckled. Richard reached over, grabbed his wife by the waist, and dragged her down to lie next to him. As the happy couple cuddled and kissed, soft morning light filtered in through their bedroom window. Even though the sun rose later during winter, it was always a welcome sight to see daylight push through the mists.

"This is very tempting, you beautiful lady, but I need to shower and shave for work," Richard said. "Will you be a dear and pop over to my parents' room, and ask if Dad needs any help with Mom?"

Richard's mother had early onset Alzheimer's. Even though Richard was a highly successful lawyer, he lived with his parents so that he could help his father out by sharing nursing duties. He was confident enough in his own independence not to feel awkward about living in the same room he'd had as a schoolboy, but that might have to change now that he was married.

Claire rolled over, sat up, and scrunched her toes into her slippers. She was wearing a long-sleeved shirt, a vest, and leggings, standard Cape Breton winter attire, but thought she had better hop into the bathroom quickly before going to help Bo Benson get his wife out of bed. After a fast face and mouth wash, Claire felt ready to face the day and anything it could throw at her. She shuffled over to the Bensons' bedroom and knocked,

"Good morning, Bo! Need any help with Brigitte today?"

"Yes, please, Claire," Bo shouted from inside the room.

Claire opened the door and went to help Mr. Benson bathe and dress his wife. She had experience handling dementia sufferers. John Havisham, her father, was a successful doctor, and he had made sure his two daughters were aware of how to treat any patient with the dignity and care they deserved. Between Bo and Claire, Brigitte Benson was soon clean and dressed and seated at her favorite place by the bay window at the front of the house.

"Are you sure you're both going to be okay while I go tell my mom about the wedding?" Claire asked, while searching online for an available car rental company.

"You go right ahead and visit your mom, Mrs. Claire Benson," Bo said with a smile, "I'm sure she'll have a million questions to ask you. But if any young couple had good reason not to have a pre-planned wedding, it has to be the both of you."

Claire nodded her head fervently in agreement and went to the dining room to make her calls.

After securing a rental vehicle, Claire went back to the bedroom she shared with Richard. "All set, honey, I'll send you a text when I arrive at the cottage."

Richard was already dressed and on his way out. He shared office space with Kate Pfeiffer, the woman who had offered him a job in Sydney when his mother's dementia had worsened. Richard looked devastatingly handsome in his perfectly fitted suit and sharply knotted tie. Claire felt a surge of attraction course through her body as he bent to kiss her goodbye.

"Thank you for helping with Mom, darling. I'll hear from you later." And with a soft brush of his lips against hers, Richard was gone.

Claire gave herself a shake and began to pack for the short visit to Pleasant Bay. She had gone a bit crazy in Las Vegas and bought herself a whole new wardrobe. Most of the clothes were day wear, but some adorable negligees and lace teddies had found their way into her shopping basket, too.

Well, why not? It was for my honeymoon, after all. And I must say that those cute black French knickers had the most interesting effect on Richard's concentration. Sadly, they must stay here until I get back.

The valet honked the car horn to let Claire know the rental was outside. One and a half hours later, Claire was disembarking at Jersey Cove and preparing to drive north along Cabot Trail Road. The Atlantic stretched to meet the chilly winter skies on her right, and mile after mile of starkly ancient Acadian forest brooded on her left. This was her favorite route. Claire turned off the podcast she'd been listening to and allowed the silence of the winter landscape to envelop her. She swung the car around gentle twists and bends in the road as it followed the sloping hills and dells carved out by the Grande Anse River.

It wasn't long before Claire began to recognize the telltale signs that the Pleasant Bay Road turnoff was approaching. A flash of ocean could be seen between the tree line. She slowed down and then turned right. Songbird Cottage would soon be in sight.

Emma's face could be seen in the window as Claire pulled into the cottage driveway. As soon as she got out of the car, Claire ran in to give her mother a long, hard hug.

"I don't know what to call you now," Emma laughed, "Miss Havisham or Mrs. Benson?"

"I'm changing over to Benson, Mom. Richard's side of the family likes to keep track of their ancestry and family tree, and if I take his name, it will make it easier for them." Claire remembered she had to apply for a new driver's license and passport. She made a mental note of it before switching on the kettle to make a mug of hot tea.

Emma was already sitting eagerly at the dining table—her eyes were agog for news. Claire sat down opposite her and began to explain the reason for their quickie marriage.

"Mom, you remember that Richard's ex-fiancée, Geneviève, came over here to try and get him back. She was a classic case of someone who doesn't mind her ex leaving, just so long as both parties stay free."

"Oh, goodness, yes. I know what you mean," Emma said, "Always having hope that the ex will come back and reality of the breakup only setting in when the ex moves on!"

"Exactly," Claire said, happy that her mom had gotten a grasp of the situation Richard and she had been facing, "she said they had a baby together, so Richard had a lab tech fly out to Montreal, and we're waiting for the paternity results."

"Yikes," Emma grimaced, "sounds like she came out with all guns blazing."

Claire couldn't help laughing. "Richard had a look through his journals and bank statements for dates and travel details, but it's just a formality so that she can't make any more false claims."

"Let me guess," Emma stated matter-of-factly, "she saw pics of you two together on social media, realized her chance of making up with Richard was not going to happen, and thought she could throw a wrench in the works."

"Sounds about right, Mom," Claire sighed.

"And this baby?" Emma was curious about how the newly married couple was going to react if the baby turned out to be Richard's.

"The dates don't add up. No baby in the world can be born after a pregnancy spanning eleven months! Here's how I read it— she had a rebound breakup fling with someone, and… well, what can I say?" Claire said as she shrugged her shoulders. "The most important thing was to let Geneviève know she hasn't a snow-ball's chance of getting back with Richard, so we got married."

Claire lifted her mug up off the table, saw a light ring of water on its old scarred surface, and began to trace its outline with her finger.

"Mom, I have to tell you something, and I don't want you to get upset."

"Yikes, that sounds ominous," Emma said with a small laugh.

Claire knew she had to tell her mother the truth about something terrible that had happened to her in the past.

Since coming to live in Songbird Cottage over six months ago, anonymous presents and flowers had started being delivered to her. Mr. Benson had helped Claire discover who it was that was sending them: her ex-stepbrother, Chuck du Pont. Chuck had heard through the grapevine that Claire had broken up with her long-term boyfriend and thought he could rekindle an interest in him that Claire had never felt in the first place. He was someone who had taken advantage of living in the same house as a beautiful teenage girl and used it for his own selfish gratification. The traumatized teenaged Claire had left the house where she had lived with her father and his new wife, Linette, and gone to live with Emma. It was the easiest way of escaping Linette and her two sons, Chippy and Chuck. She had kept the reason for her flight a secret from her mother, but now it was time to tell her.

Claire held Emma's hands tightly over the table as she told her sad story. Emma's face went alternately white with shock and then red with rage.

"So, you see, Mom, I had to get married. I sent a few wedding photos of me and Richard from Las Vegas to the person who was telling Chuck details about my life, and I don't expect to ever hear from him again. Sometimes that ring on the finger is the *only* thing that people understand, don't you think?"

Emma had tears flooding her eyes, but she nodded sorrowfully and squeezed her daughter's hand.

Claire perked up, "Come on, Mom, don't feel bad. I'm happy, in love, and married—and guess what? It's time for you to plan the wedding reception of the century for me and Richard, right here at Songbird Cottage!"

Chapter Two: Spring Parties Are the Best

The phone vibrated—either late at night or early in the morning—Claire wasn't sure which. Fumbling for her device, she eventually located it by looking for the pulsing, rattling neon glow and pushed the green icon.

"Izzy, what the—are you okay?" It was Isabelle Havisham, Claire's young sister.

"Sooorry, but in New York this is considered to be a normal time to call a beloved sister, Claire Bear. Just wanted to see how you were doing…" Izzy sounded excited and breathless, and Claire sat up and turned on her end table light. She could see the spring day's dawn slowly coloring the horizon outside, a velvety gray. A few songbirds were tuning their voices in the trees for the full sunrise chorus.

"Mom's got everything under control, Izzy. She's been as busy as a bee since winter, planning this party. It would be great if you could come over sometime, though, and try on the dress she's had made for you."

Claire could hear strange sounds in the background of Izzy's phone call: the thump of a song's bass line, static sounds of the phone earpiece rubbing against Izzy's hair as though she were pacing up and down, her heavy breathing, panting, the occasional sniff.

"Are you okay, little sis? You sound as though you're running a marathon." Claire thought something sounded a bit off. And why on earth was Izz calling at this forsaken hour of the morning?

"Everything's fine, don't get on your high horse—it's not that late, early, whatever." Izzy gave another sniff. "If you really want me to come, I can. It's just that I need a little help with my transportation. I wanna fly, and Dad won't pay for a ticket. And before you tell me I can travel by bus or train or something just as crazy, let me add that if I can't fly, then I'm not coming."

Claire frowned and sat up a bit straighter in bed. She plumped her pillows out behind her and gave the luminous digits on her watch a glance. It was four thirty in the morning. Something was not right.

"That doesn't sound like Dad at all. Why won't he pay?" Claire had to get to the bottom of this.

Izzy swore loudly, and Claire pulled her ear away from the phone. "He won't pay for my ticket 'cause I lost my job as a courier, and he's mad."

Claire waited. There was always more with Izzy, and she knew all she had to do was wait.

"And I owe him some money; at least I borrowed some money from him, but it's his fault for not just giving it to me, the old miser." Izzy gave another sniff.

Claire had heard these words coming from Izzy since her younger sister had dropped out of her last college course. Both Havisham girls had been brought up to make it in the world on their own and never to rely on their wealthy father for handouts. The only leg-up they had ever received was an apartment of their choice up to a certain dollar amount. Claire's apartment in Bangor, Maine, was earning her a steady income as a rental, and Izzy still lived in the Manhattan apartment she had chosen for herself. But it seemed to Claire that Izzy had a decidedly unfair advantage when it came to their father's money. Isabelle always had full use of one of Dr. John Havisham's credit cards and unlimited access to his various accounts. It was hard to calculate, but Claire gauged that Izzy's hectically bohemian New York lifestyle cost upwards of two thousand dollars a month over and above what she earned as a courier and nighttime rock band singer.

That reminded Claire of something. "Hey Izz, don't you think you should turn your music down a touch? Your co-op has some pretty draconian by-laws about after-hours noise levels."

"Forget those old fogies," Izzy slurred slightly. The phone line went mute for a second or two, and then Izzy's voice came back in focus. After regaining her ability to concentrate, Izzy begged, "Listen, Claire, please can you send me some money for a ticket to come over and visit? I will pay you back 'cause I start a new courier job next week, and my band is playing a gig. It's only to tide me over until then. Pleeeeease."

Claire knew their mother was set on Izzy trying on the gorgeous dress she'd had specially designed for her, and with the party date rapidly approaching, this needed to be sooner rather than later. She didn't want to upset Emma by acting churlishly towards her sister. She had to make allowances for the erratic behavior of someone who lived a night owl existence in that twenty-four-hour beehive called Manhattan.

"Okay, I'll send you five hundred dollars via my banking app when I'm more awake in the morning. Now, will you go to sleep and reset your body clock before getting here, please? Everyone will think it very strange of you, Izz, if you are still bouncing around at sunrise in Cape Breton."

"Can you make it one thousand, please, please, pretty please?" Izzy implored.

"Yes, okay, goodbye." Claire hung up, but not before hearing her sister give a long sniff into the receiver.

I hope she doesn't give me that nasty cold when she arrives. Goodness knows I don't want my party photos showing me all feverish and sick.

And with those thoughts in her mind, Claire drifted off back to sleep. The melodic chirps of songbirds at dawn filtered down from the trees and in through the open windows. The transition from nature's nocturnal noises to early morning daytime sounds were the last thing she heard before dreams overtook her.

Claire woke several hours later. It was strange to think of Richard waking up all alone without her on the other side of the island. She missed his warmth and the sound of him breathing at night but took comfort in the fact that when she saw him at their "better late than never" wedding lunch, it would be worth the wait.

Claire was staying at Songbird Cottage to help Emma get the final arrangements done. Both of them were very excited. Spring parties were the best, and this one would hopefully prove to be as memorable as if it were a real wedding reception. All the food was being locally sourced, and with spring so far advanced, they could look forward to a cornucopia of fresh vegetables and produce. The cottage's garden was liberally peppered with red, silver, and sugar maple trees and their fuzzy flowers had only recently given way to a riot of lime green, ketchup red, and metallic silver foliage. The buckets hooked to the tree trunks for sap collection had been taken down and the contents transported to Sam's brewery next door. Every drop of sap had already been boiled down and bottled, ready for shipping out to Sam's customers all over the world.

The morning wasn't very far advanced when Claire heard the sound of Emma's little hatchback pull into the driveway. She saw her mother walk around the back of the car and begin unloading boxes of pickling jars that had handles added to them to create beer mugs. She walked outside to go and help.

"You're up bright and early this morning, Mom," Claire noted as she picked up a crate of pickling jars. "I had the strangest call from Izz a few hours ago," she commented as the two of them walked back inside and dumped the boxes onto the old wooden dining table that stood in the middle of the cottage. "She wanted —no, needed—one thousand dollars for plane fare to get here and for other sundries I'm presuming."

Emma was unpacking the mason jar mugs onto the table and inspecting them for fingerprints and dust, but she stopped what she was doing after Claire finished talking.

"That's very interesting, Bear," Emma replied with an inscrutable look on her face, "because she also asked me for the same thing only a few days ago, and Sam says Izzy also hit him up for a loan early last week."

They looked at each other across the table; the boxes between them on the table lay forgotten for a moment. With a sigh, Emma deduced, "It sounds as though Izzy has gotten herself into some kind of trouble. I wonder what it is, this time. Running up her accounts, crashing a friend's van, buying an expensive piece of music equipment?"

Emma had just recited a list of things Izzy had done in the

past.

Claire returned to unpacking the boxes. "The thing is, Mom, she's almost thirty years old now, and these—what does Dad call them again, 'little peccadillos'—shouldn't be happening anymore. What were understandable teenage shenanigans morphed into youthful twenty-something rebellion, but now it's just unacceptable adult behavior—and I'm sick of it, quite frankly."

Emma took a tray of the mugs to the kitchenette sink, which she began to fill with soapy hot water. She stayed quiet while the water was running and then replied after turning the faucet off, "She had an awful cold last week when she called me, and that means she's probably not looking after herself very well."

"She still has the sniffles," Claire added, "and she's probably taking one of those horrid cold medications that has ephedrine in it because she was really amped up this morning. I've always wished she wasn't so selfish and self-absorbed, but Izz has some sweet characteristics that used to make up for it."

Emma smiled as she came back to the table, wiping her wet hands on a dishcloth. "I know what you mean, Bear. She can be so kind and helpful when she wants to be. I remember how you both came through for me after my second husband died,"—after nearly two years, Emma still couldn't say the name of the man who had stolen all her life savings before suddenly dying from a heart attack—"but recently, I've seen an escalation in her money borrowing and phone calls at all hours of the day and night."

"I'm going to speak to her when she comes for her dress fitting," Claire stated determinedly, "because she won't be able to duck and dive us when she's back here at Songbird Cottage."

Chapter Three: A Box of Frogs

Izzy's rental car parked erratically on the curb at the end of the Songbird Cottage driveway the next day.

"Bring it in and park it closer to the cottage, Izz," Claire shouted down to her sister as Izzy loped toward her, hefting her duffle bag.

"Nope, thanks. It's fine where it is, and I hate it when people wait until someone is out of their car before telling them to go back in and move it," Izzy said, giving her big sister a big hug. The faint whiff of cheap airplane wine hung in the air after Izzy had walked through the front door. She saw that Claire had taken up residence in their mother's old mezzanine level bedroom. "So, I get to sleep downstairs in our old bedroom now, do I? That's great 'cause then I don't have to go up and down those stupid narrow steps when I need to visit the bathroom."

Izzy disappeared into the small guest bedroom and closed the door behind her. Claire switched on the kettle for some tea but decided to change it to coffee after realizing Izzy would probably need something warm and sobering if she had spent her flight drinking. She hoped she had kept her alcohol consumption to within the two-drink maximum for driving. Claire didn't like the idea of bailing her sister out after driving under the influence charges had been made against her.

Izzy came out of the bedroom and went over to the bathroom. Claire heard the sound of the shower running and turned off the kettle. It would be a while before Izzy would emerge from the bathroom, and Claire knew the coffee would be cold by then. She took out her phone and planned on spending the waiting time texting her mom and Richard: the first, to tell her that Izzy had arrived and the second, to tell him she loved and missed him.

About half an hour later, Izzy came out of the bathroom. Her hair smelled of Claire's peaches and herb shampoo and conditioner, and her breath smelled of mint toothpaste. Claire couldn't help but breathe a sigh of relief. She didn't want their mother worrying about the stale wine fumes Izzy had been giving off when she'd arrived.

"I texted Mom from the bathroom to let her know I'd arrived," Izzy said and went to the fridge. She took out one of the beers Sam left there for guests and opened it.

"So did I," Claire replied and gave up on the hope that Izzy would smell nice for their mother. She watched as Izzy quickly downed her beer and then took another out of the fridge before closing its door.

As if speaking of angels, Emma drove up right then and parked next to the front door. That only meant one thing—she had a trunk full of boxes she needed to unload again. Claire smiled.

It would be much easier for Mom to borrow Sam's SUV and do all her transporting in one trip, but I guess she's chosen to do it this way so she can visit more frequently. She knows I'm moving across the island permanently after the party, and this is her way of spending time with me—and with Songbird Cottage.

It was sad to think of the little cottage being empty after Claire moved out. Maybe she should speak to her mother about turning it into an Airbnb or something. They would have to clear it with their father first, though. He was super-cautious about insurance coverage.

"Hi my lovely girls!" Emma was always happy to have her family reunited. It made her feel young again to have her two daughters with her. "Izzy, my special little girl, how are you? How's that cold?"

Izzy grinned at Emma after accepting her enthusiastic embrace. "What cold, Mom? I'm fine. Where's that dress? Let's get this fitting over and done with." Claire noticed Izzy seemed to be in a much better mood now that she had some alcohol inside of her.

Emma looked around and found an old paper boutique bag she'd brought in with her. She handed it to Izzy, saying, "You can put it on in here, sweetie. No one's around except me and Claire. I need to check the length for it to be hemmed in time. Wait! Let me get the shoes to go with it."

Izzy opened the bag and pulled out a diaphanous gossamer creation. Layer after layer of jacket, shirt, T-shirt, and jeans were removed before Izzy could pull the dress on over her head. The dress floated to her heels with a light ripple. Claire and Emma stepped back to better observe. Izzy bent over to kick off her boots and slip on the pumps Emma had bought to go with the outfit.

When Izzy stood up straight and did a twirl to show off how the dress flared around her ankles, Claire found it hard to know whether to laugh or cry. Her little sister looked like a scarecrow that had had a large semi-transparent plastic bag blow over and stick to it. Only now, in the cold light of day, was it possible for Claire see how much weight Izzy had lost. Her skin looked sallow and spotty, her elbows poked out at her sides like acute angles, and her shoulder blades and collar bones protruded out almost further than the rest of her body.

Claire turned to see what kind of effect this was having on their mother. Emma was standing, staring at Izzy, her mind turning in circles to find a way to express her emotions diplomatically.

"Um, maybe it's the wet hair that's making it look so gauche," Emma started off saying, then she abandoned all pretense at euphemisms, "you've lost so much weight, Izz! What have you been doing over there? I'm very tempted to take a photo of you and send it to your father! He's here in Cape Breton, you realize. He's docked at the Marina."

Izzy sat down on the low brown velvet sofa that had been squashed into a corner of the cottage since forever. She took out a packet of cigarettes and fished one out to light. Izzy had always enjoyed smoking with her friends at nightclubs and gigs, but this was the first her family knew about her graduating to occupational smoking.

Emma gave a shriek when Izzy lit the cigarette and inhaled deeply.

"Take off the dress, my goodness! One flake of ash could have the whole thing go up in one big flame. When did you start this nonsense?"

"First my weight, and now my smoking. Stop giving me the first degree, Mom. I'm old enough to make my own decisions about my body."

Izzy sat glowering up at Claire and Emma as she sat on the sofa. She made no move to take off the dress.

"I'll get you an ashtray, shall I?" Claire said and moved to the kitchenette to find one of the ashtrays they kept there for guests.

When she turned around, Emma was busy trying to get the dress off Izzy while her daughter nonchalantly transferred her cigarette from one hand to the other. Claire thought back to how excited her mom had been looking at dress designs and fabrics, working hard to find the perfect match for her youngest daughter's avant garde appearance. It seemed as though somewhere along the line, Izzy had changed more than anyone could have expected. Claire felt sad for Emma and mad at Izzy.

Claire moved to sit at the table opposite Izzy and slammed the ashtray down in front of her. "There's your ashtray, you ungrateful brat!" Claire wanted to give Izzy the wake-up call she'd been preparing for her sister from the time she'd arrived. "Does it even cross your self-centered mind that you've ruined Mom's treat? Yes, don't roll your eyes at me like that. While you've been stuck in your wasteful life, living your stupid metropolitan lifestyle enabled by our parents' money, Mom has been slaving away trying to make you something nice, something special just for you. It's handed to you on a silver platter, just like everything else has always been handed to you, and you don't even have the decency to be grateful."

Izzy sat up as straight as she was able to, from deep within the voluminous velvet cushions. "Shut up, Miss Priss! You think you're so perfect because you're married, and you got a college degree. I have more talent in my little finger than you have in your entire body."

"Girls, girls!" Emma was aghast; she hadn't seen Claire and Izzy fight since they were teenagers sharing a room in her Tribeca apartment. "Please don't shout at each other. I don't care about the dress; let Isabelle wear whatever she wants."

Claire put her hand up in an arresting gesture, "No, Mom, that's what you and Dad always do. You back down and let her have her own way all the time. Well, it's got to stop."

"I don't have to listen to this," Izzy said, struggling out of the sofa and standing up. She ground her cigarette out in the ashtray. "I'm going back to Manhattan where I can wear what I like. Forget your stupid spring party or whatever this sorry excuse for blatant consumerism is!" She stormed out of the cottage living area and slammed the guest room door behind her.

Emma burst into tears. She hated conflict and had striven to choose the high road all her life, rather than squabble and bicker. Claire was immediately sorry her mother was upset and went to comfort her.

"Just give her time to settle down, Mom, and once she's gotten over her sulks, I'm sure she'll give the dress another try," Claire said in a light, optimistic tone.

"But I planned on having Sam come over this evening and everyone having fresh pizza made in the old pottery kiln," Emma sniffed, wiping her eyes with the back of her hands. "We were all meant to drive to Halifax tomorrow and pick up Sam's sons from the airport."

As she spoke, Izzy burst out of the guest room, duffle bag in one hand and an empty beer bottle in the other. She stopped at the fridge, put the empty bottle on top, and bent to take another beer out of the fridge side door. Then she kicked the fridge closed with her foot and walked to the front door. "Later, losers," she said, "have fun explaining to Dad why I'm not here 'cause I already texted to tell him that you are mean, narrow-minded witches."

Emma and Claire could only stare in confusion as Izzy walked out. Claire came to her senses first and ran after her sister. "Izzy, please, you can't drink and drive! Please let me call you a cab, or Sam can drive you to Halifax."

Izzy threw her bag into the backseat, gave Claire the middle finger, reversed crazily off the curb, and screeched off down the road. Claire lost no time in calling Sam and telling him what had happened.

"I'll be there in a second," Sam said, and true to his word, the sound of his SUV coming to Songbird Cottage could be heard three minutes later. The craft beer brewery where he and Emma lived was only a couple of hundred yards down the road.

Sam leaned out of his SUV window and asked Claire, "You want I go after her?"

Claire gave it some thought, and then shook her head. "No, Sam, thanks for the offer, but she made it all the way here in one piece. We can only hope she does the same going back. Mom's inside crying."

That was all that Sam needed to hear. He had loved Emma unconditionally since they had first met over twenty years ago. It had taken a while for their paths to cross and intertwine, but now that they had, Sam was adamant that nothing bad would ever happen to his wife ever again. He drove up to the cottage door, parked behind the hatchback, and went inside.

Sam found Emma wiping her eyes with a thin tissue she had taken from a box on the credenza in the corner. It looked as though she'd been hit by a miniature emotional hurricane. The dress lay in a crumpled ball on her lap, and bits of the tissue she'd used to wipe her face were stuck to her cheeks and nose.

Sam moved to take Emma in his arms. "Sweetheart, nothing is worth this misery. Tell me what happened, and I swear I will do everything in my power to make things right."

Emma told her husband every detail of her youngest daughter's actions since her arrival at Songbird Cottage less than an hour before. When she had finished, Claire came to sit down next to the couple and filled them in on Izzy's inconsistent behavior before their mother's arrival.

"Quite frankly, she acted as crazy as a box of frogs, guys," Claire said with a frown. "It was hard to work out if she was in a good mood or a bad one. I think we should tell Dad to send her for a psyche evaluation. Izzy is a piece of work!"

Chapter Four: Secrets and Lies

Sam sat in quiet contemplation for a few minutes. Then he patted Emma's knee comfortingly and reached over to brush a few remaining bits of tissue off her face.

"I think we can stay here tomorrow, and I'll tell the boys to drive up to Pleasant Bay in a couple of rentals. It's a better idea anyway because then they'll have their own transportation during their stay," Sam said quietly.

Claire raised an eyebrow. It seemed to her as though Sam had missed the point of Izzy's unacceptable conduct, completely.

"I'm going to ask Luke to catch a flight over to New York from Halifax, instead of joining us here right away. He can bring Isabelle back to Cape Breton with him. They chat online occasionally, and he should be able to make her see some sense." Sam kept his eyes on Emma while he said this and was encouraged by her giving a slight smile when she heard his plan.

Luke was Sam's youngest son. His three boys had grown up overseas in South Africa. A brief holiday romance and quickie wedding with their mother, a South African hoping to make Canada her new home, had ended in failure, but not before the couple had had three sons in quick succession. The divorce had been rough, with Sam not quite trusting the artifice of peace and stability South Africa portrayed to the media, and there had been a lot of fighting to keep his boys with him in Cape Breton.

Sam settled on having them during every school vacation, but by the time his sons had become grown men, they were already firmly entrenched in the South African way of life. His two eldest sons, Roscoe and Thurston, were happily married and working in Cape Town. They were bringing their wives with them on this visit. Luke, the youngest, worked on a sheep farm in the middle of the arid Karoo desert. He had no plans yet to settle down and seemed the most likely out of Sam's children to follow in his father's footsteps and return to live in Pleasant Bay.

Sam stood up, "Well, I think that's everything done and dusted here for now, Claire. Would you be a dear and come to pick up the rest of the decorations and glassware at the brewery today?"

"Sure thing, Sam," Claire acquiesced gladly to Sam's plan. It would give her something to do for the rest of the day and would also allow Emma to spend time preparing the spare rooms at the brewery for Sam's sons and their wives.

Just then, the phone next to Emma's old work desk gave a shrill ring. It was a fairly rare occurrence, as Songbird Cottage had been unoccupied for the main part, since Claire spent a considerable portion of her time with Richard in Sydney. Folks who stayed here intermittently always asked people to call on their mobile phones instead.

Claire picked up the landline phone, "Hello, Claire speaking," she said hesitantly, secretly hoping it was Izzy calling to apologize and ask if she could come back of her own volition.

"What's going on over there? Izzy says you are acting irrationally and that she had to leave because you were bullying her." It was Dr. John Havisham, Claire and Izzy's father. He sounded angry.

Claire's eyes widened in shock. "What!? No! That's not what happened, Dad!"

John Havisham didn't sound mollified in the slightest. "She told me you'd act all innocent, Claire, but she says she had to leave because your mother and you were both body shaming her, criticizing her musical talents, and all sorts of backbiting nonsense you know I can't stand."

"Hang on Dad, Mom and Sam are here. I'm putting you on speaker." Claire pushed the microphone button, hung up the receiver, and went to sit down next to her mother.

"Emma, you there? Why have you allowed Claire to victimize Isabelle? She tells me you were just sitting there and allowing it to happen. She had no choice but to leave, and I'm on her side because why should she sit there and take your abuse?" John was very angry. He had been enjoying a peaceful morning on his yacht at the Marina, and Izzy's texts and phone call had ruined his serenity. "I allow you two to stay in my cottage out of the kindness of my heart, but if this is how you choose to use it, then I want all sets of keys back!"

John had hated hearing his two daughters bickering when he had been a single parent and had been secretly delighted when the teenage girls had opted to go and stay with their mother in Manhattan and only visit him over weekends. He could be incredibly irascible on the odd occasion, especially when it came to his downtime being disturbed.

Emma opened her mouth to reply, but no words came out. The unfairness of it all had taken away her ability to talk.

"Er...hey buddy, it's Sam here. Emma has got a bit of a sore throat, so maybe that's why everyone came off a little cranky today. Still, no harm done, what do you think?"

Emma and Claire looked at Sam as though he were a guardian angel. The phone line was silent, and the listeners at Songbird Cottage heard the sound of John closing a door and sitting down in a creaking wicker chair.

"Hi, Sam, thanks for holding down the fort there until the party. I'll definitely be attending with Kate, so let's hope that everyone can just get along until then, hey?"

"That won't be a problem, John. I'm sending Luke over to New York when he arrives tomorrow, and he's going to pick up Isabelle and accompany her back here in time for the party. Sound good?"

They heard the sound of John taking a sip of drink and then the sound of the glass being put back down on a table. "Yeah, that's a good idea. I've put another couple of thousand dollars into Izzy's bank account, so she should have enough to pay for two tickets back out here, with the exchange rate and all."

"Any reason why Izzy couldn't stay in the Halifax house, or is your soon-to-be ex-wife Linette still there? It would save us all the flying back and forth to the Big Apple."

John gave a pause to think, before replying, "No, actually, the house is empty. Linette's already parlayed some of her settlement into buying a nice piece of real estate on the Upper East Side. I don't know why Izzy can't stay there in Halifax."

"Could you send her a text and ask her?" Claire knew that Izzy would only bother answering messages her father sent her. Isabelle Havisham had always been skilled at cajoling John to see her side of the story.

"Hang on, I'll do it now."

Once again, they heard the sound of John taking a sip of his drink and then a few beeps while he sent a message. They all waited to see if Izzy would reply.

Claire got up and went to switch on the kettle. She had a vision of Izzy driving along the curving Cabot Trail Road, one hand gripping a beer bottle and the other hand answering her text messages, holding the steering wheel steady with her knee. Claire shuddered and made herself a strong cup of instant coffee.

A few more beeps were heard, and then John obviously placed his phone back against his ear. "Okay, she says she's flying back to New York, something to do with feeling safe there, or something." John sounded relieved he wouldn't have to worry about Izzy staying at the Northwest Arm Halifax mansion. She had a bad habit of trashing a place.

"No worries, John, Luke will enjoy the chance to check out Manhattan again. Take care, and see you soon," Sam said as he signaled to Claire that she could disconnect the line. The last thing they heard was John taking another long swig of his drink.

Claire sighed, "Like father, like daughter," she said.

"What do you mean, Claire?" Emma asked, "I've never seen your father drink more than three beers in an afternoon, and from what I can see from all the empty bottles on top of the fridge, Izzy managed to get through that number in less than half an hour."

Sam stood up, "Let's get going, honey." He turned to Claire before he walked out of the door, "See you later at the brewery—I'll get another six-pack ready for you to restock the fridge."

Claire gave him a thumbs up and watched Sam escort Emma to her hatchback, open the door, and then close it gently after her. He strode to the SUV, hopped inside, and reversed smoothly away with her mother's little hatchback scurrying after him.

Claire sighed and turned away from the window. She walked

thoughtfully over to the fridge and stood staring at the empty beer bottles on top of it. Then she ambled slowly down the couple of stairs that led down to the bathroom. It was still damp and slightly steamy in there. Two wet towels sat in a puddle of water next to the shower. The toothpaste cap was off, and a worm of mint toothpaste was oozing out onto the sink. Claire wiped down the shower and sink with the two wet towels and placed them in the dirty laundry basket in the corner. They could wait until that evening when she would run a wash cycle in the kitchenette.

Claire's next stop was the guest room. The drapes had been tightly drawn to block out the sunlight. Hoping she didn't stub her toes against anything, Claire navigated her way over to the window and drew back the drapes. It illuminated the guest room like a spotlight. She saw the two little twin beds where Izzy and she had slept and played as children all those years ago. The multicolored rag rugs on the floor, the miniature pipe cleaner statues, the seashells, and smooth wave-rounded stones they had picked up on the beach. Each one had been fallen in love with, and the two small girls had insisted upon bringing them home —there, the eclectic items sat faithfully as time sped by, in the exact spots where they had been placed all those years ago. A lump came into her throat when she saw the dust and cobwebs that stuck to these once treasured mementoes.

Then Claire's eye caught sight of something that didn't belong in the room. On top of the chest of drawers in the corner, next to an ancient bowl of withered flowers that adorned its wooden surface, was a large gap in the dust. As Claire moved closer, she could see the dust had been wiped off by the outline of a small handprint. The remnants of a fine white powder had been placed on the clean space. Next to the few grains of white powder that had been left behind, there was a plastic straw, cut in half to make it shorter.

Claire had watched enough police shows on her streaming service to know what to do. She dipped her finger into her mouth, wet the tip of it, and dabbed it on the powder. Then she rubbed the powder onto her gums.

Claire's gums went numb. She held her breath and waited.

The feeling that overcame her was so subtle, so insidious, that Claire wasn't quite sure if it had begun or even when it began. She felt a lift, a kick, and tug of her mood. Her mind expanded with hope, focus, and exhilaration. Whatever she had been feeling oppressed or depressed about no longer mattered. She experienced a desire to run around and read, write, create, talk, dance, and do the housework all at once.

Yes, there was no longer any doubt about it.

Izzy was doing drugs.

Chapter Five: The Party

Claire called Richard after she'd discovered cocaine in the room where Izzy had stayed for a less than an hour. He took the news calmly.

"I'm not shocked, and nor should you be, darling," he said evenly, "she hangs with a crowd of people who are all probably okay with the concept of drugs, if not the actual use of them. I'm surprised it hasn't happened sooner. How old is she now?"

"Izzy's a couple years younger than I am. She's almost thirty." Claire had to fight the urge to be judgmental, but like all well-balanced people, she struggled to understand addiction.

"When did you check up on her, make sure she's living a happy and connected life? She lost her job, which is a big sign. Addiction comes easier to those who don't have a reason to get up in the mornings."

Claire paused; she hadn't been to visit Izzy for many, many months. She knew Emma hadn't either. Even when their own lives had gotten firmly back on track, Emma and Claire hadn't made the time to reach out to Izzy in New York, either by calling or messaging her.

"Your silence tells me everything I need to know," Richard commented in a neutral tone.

Claire bristled in defense of herself and her mother, "That's unfair, Richard! How are Mom and I expected to play nursemaid to someone nearly thirty years of age, when we have had huge problems of our own to solve?"

"Darling, I see you texting and commenting on social media in bed every night at home. Are you telling me that none of them were to Izzy?" Richard was determined to shine a light on those people who were meant to keep Izzy in their thoughts.

Claire didn't know how to defend herself against what she considered to be unfair accusations. How could she explain that it was easier to chat with her old school friends and the women with whom she'd attended college? They were all married or in a serious relationship and understood her aspirations and goals. Whereas, whenever Claire called Izzy or messaged her, only two outcomes would arise from it; either Izzy was too busy to reply or too tired to chat. It had been a dead end. And Izzy always called back or messaged at completely unacceptable hours. She had surmised this was because she didn't have to get up for work in the mornings.

Claire told this to Richard.

Richard heard her out and then said, "Well, there's your first clue. She obviously can only call or message when she's artificially enabled by stimulants. Did she sound on point at these times?"

Claire replied slowly, "Noooo, she would sound slurry, and her speech patterns would be inconsistent."

Richard retained his composure. "Let's hope poor Luke can get her here and keep her on a leash during the party. Your mom has put a lot of effort into this, and I wouldn't want it ruined for her sake. Don't tell anyone your suspicions yet. Wait until after, okay?"

The couple blew kisses through the phone, and Claire hung up after telling Richard she loved and missed him.

Claire didn't have time to dwell on what Richard had said. She spent the next day driving back and forth from the brewery to the cottage. Soon, the living area at Songbird Cottage was filled with boxes of tableware and crates of china. Everyone was waiting for Roscoe and Thurston, Sam's two eldest sons, to recover from jetlag so that they could help with setting up the tables and chairs. Claire and Emma couldn't stop opening up their weather apps to check for rain, and they were reassured by sunshine icons every time. Excitement started to build as friends and family began to arrive at surrounding neighborhood bed and breakfasts. The texts telling Claire or Emma everyone was busy unpacking and resting after their trip came flooding in, and their phones chimed and chirped like over-enthusiastic birds.

This is what our family needs after so many bad things happening to us over the last two years. I want to acknowledge our stability and success just as much as I want to celebrate my marriage to Richard.

Claire knew better than to suggest to Sam that his family dine with her on the day she saw the two fully loaded rental vehicles drive past Songbird Cottage. His sons and their wives would be jaded after flying all the way from Cape Town. Her heart went out to Luke, who would have to continue his journey on to JFK. They had factored in how long it would take all the guests to feel better after traveling and had set the date of the party for one day thereafter. This gave Emma and Claire two days to get the garden looking as spectacular as they had envisioned.

The yard didn't need that much help—nature had already supplied most of the beauty. The garden was abloom with mauve mayflowers, wild leek, and spring beauties. Pushing through the side of the cottage boundaries, Dutchman's breeches and toothwort poked through the hedges. Emma and Claire had hiked a short way through the hardwood forest earlier that day and picked trout lilies and wild sarsaparilla to place in bud vases on the tables. They had returned with their heads clear and smiles on their faces. There was nothing to beat an early morning walk in the forest.

By eleven o' clock, the cottage was a hive of activity. Roscoe, Thurston, and Sam were busy setting out the long trestle tables, chairs, and benches. Emma and Claire then spread linen tablecloths over them and lay small tin buckets of cutlery and piles of plates on top. A vase of spring flowers was placed at each end, and a paper napkin holder completed the presentation. Roscoe and Thurston's wives sat inside the Cottage, sipping on glasses of chilled white wine, chatting about what they wanted to buy and take back to Cape Town with them. They weren't used to doing housework or party preparation, as they had staff back home in South Africa who did all of that kind of stuff for them.

Everyone in the garden cocked their heads and listened when they heard the sound of a vehicle approaching.

"I can't believe you live so far off the beaten track here that everyone thinks it's a major event when a car drives past," Roscoe's wife, Tarryn, commented to Emma, as Claire's mother scrubbed the inside of the old pottery kiln. "I had to sleep with the fan on in our room last night because I found the dead silence so disturbing," she noted as she took another sip of her wine.

"If you lived here, you'd soon get used to it," Emma said with a smile. "A friend of mine who went to Cape Town on vacation said she couldn't sleep because the sound of police sirens kept her awake all night, so it's horses for courses, isn't it?"

Tarryn scoffed, "Your friend's lucky she didn't get carjacked, Emma, then she would be grateful for the sound of sirens."

The two women watched as Luke's rental car pulled up to the curb outside. He knew to leave the driveway clear, with room for guests' cars on either side. Izzy stepped out of the rental, left Luke to carry in her bag, and walked up to where Emma and Claire stood with welcoming smiles on their faces. They hoped to keep Izzy happy until her father arrived.

"Hello, you lot!" Izzy was cheerful and conveniently forgetful as well. "I am so pleased I arrived just late enough to avoid all this"—she gestured at all the preparations going on around her —"but early enough to have a glass of wine."

Izzy gave her sister and mother a brief hug and walked into the cottage. Sam had walked to the driveway entrance to see if his youngest son needed help with luggage. Luke went to meet his father halfway and gave him an affectionate greeting. "Hi Dad," he said as he gave Sam a hard hug. "I missed this place so much. Don't worry, there's not much to carry. My suitcase came up in Thurston's car, and Izzy just shoved some stuff into this backpack."

Sam made eye contact with Luke. His youngest son looked steadily back at him and gave a subtle nod of his head. Understanding registered on Sam's face, and he acknowledged Luke's silent communication.

The two men went inside the cottage. Luke went towards the small guest bedroom underneath the main mezzanine level bedroom. "Hey, Izzy, I've got your backpack here. Can I come in?" he asked as he gave a gentle tap on the door.

"Hang on! I just need to make myself gorgeous," Izzy shouted out from inside the room.

Sam stepped forward. "I'm coming in Izzy. This backpack is heavy!"

He turned the doorknob, but it was locked. The sound of drawers shutting quickly could be heard inside.

"Hang on! I said hang on!" Izzy's sweet voice had changed on a dime, and now she sounded irritable and accusatory.

The door was unlocked after a few minutes, and Izzy stood in the entrance, her hands on her hips. "What if I'd been changing in there, for goodness' sake. Have a little patience, why don't you?"

Sam was sanguine. "I apologize, Izzy, but I knew there was no chance of you 'changing in there' because I have your bag of clothes in my hand."

Izzy pushed past Sam and Luke. "I need some wine. You can put my backpack on one of the beds."

The men watched Izzy pour half a bottle of wine into a beer mug in the kitchenette and walk out to where the guests were gathering. Then they stepped into the little bedroom. Sam laid the backpack on the bed and said to Luke, "Let's have a look in the dresser drawers. We can sift through the backpack afterwards."

Sam had suspected Izzy was on drugs a few weeks back. The late-night phone calls, the requests to borrow large amounts of money, the inability to keep a job, the gradual weight loss. He had seen it all before—he had seen it all happen with Luke.

Luke and Sam rifled through the drawers. They found Izzy's straw and a balled-up square of white paper. "Looks like she's already finished the contents inside this bindle," Luke said sadly. "I'm sorry Dad. I tried to keep her under observation the whole time, but it was impossible—ladies' bathrooms and all that."

"I remember how it was with you," Sam said with a sad smile, "your mother used to despair of being able to keep you with her all the time. It's even harder with teenagers, believe me, because there's a certain expectation of free time."

Sam shrugged, "Yeah, Dad, but it helps keep your mind off drugs if you have someone to talk to and hang out with. Drug use always starts off as an experiment with loads of friends around but somehow ends up being continued at home alone with no one there to distract the demons in your head. Loneliness and lack of purpose definitely compel someone to do drugs, more than any chemical hook."

"We better get back to the party outside before Emma starts to think I'm slacking off and leaving her there to meet and greet alone. Hopefully, Richard has arrived by now and we can start the barbecue."

"Sure, Dad," Luke said, "Izzy probably has her stash in her purse or pockets. Let's get out of here."

Chapter Six: The Aftermath

J ohn closed the small guest bedroom door quietly behind him and said to the anxious group of people standing in the cottage's living area, "She should sleep it off now. I've propped her up with pillows so she can't roll onto her back and injected her with an intermuscular antinauseant. She's heavily sedated, and I might have to set up a saline solution drip with ten percent glucose and some vitamin C and B complex later, just to try and get her back on her feet."

Emma was sitting at the dining room table and tugged on Claire's sleeve. Her eldest daughter, who was seated next to her, stood up. "Everyone, thank you for staying and helping. Dad—John—has everything under control. We appreciate your concern and have all of your phone numbers, so I'm going to set up a chat group to let everyone know how Izzy fares after tonight. Okay?"

There were murmurs and whispers among the twenty or so people who had stayed behind to see if they could help. A few voices were raised, offering helpful advice:

"The 'heretohelp' website says she should eat certain foods to rebalance her serotonin."

"Narcotics Anonymous says she has to reach rock bottom before you can help her."

Claire held up her hands. "Mom's gotten all the website links you sent her, and I think that if this isn't rock bottom, then I don't know what is. Thanks again for your concern." She motioned to Richard, and he stepped forward to usher all of the remaining guests out of the cottage front door.

John Havisham collapsed into the low-level velvet sofa's soft cushions and groaned, "My reputation is ruined! How am I ever going to live down the humiliation of not noticing my own daughter is a crackhead?"

The sound of guests' cars driving off into the night was the only answer he got.

Claire's little sister had demonstrated very clearly to her parents that all was not right in Izzyland. The party had been too tempting an opportunity for her to try and find the perfect balance between alcohol consumption and drug use. From the time she had downed her second beer mug of wine to the moment she had inhaled some of her vomit during her drunken collapse in the sunken bathroom, Izzy had made it very obvious she was suffering from a dependence on harmful substances.

Claire and Emma inwardly cringed as they remembered the last seven hours they'd had to endure in Izzy's company. She had bounced from small gathering to chatting group, dominating every conversation, and loudly interrupting other people's narratives. During the delicious late afternoon lunch, Izzy had not touched a single morsel of food, but jumped from table to table, beer mug full of wine in her hand, blowing cigarette smoke inadvertently into people's faces and being incredibly witty. At least, that's what she'd thought. As the afternoon had progressed, Izzy's banter had become increasingly off-color.

"I don't know how you can bear living in Halifax, no, where do you live again? Cape Town?"

"I live in Bangor, Maine, actually, Izzy. I was one of the free-lance beauticians who worked at your sister's salon there."

"Eeww…I mean, that's even worse! You should move to Manhattan; that's the only place to live. It's got life, y'know. Can't understand how you can stay in those wretched holes. Hey! Listen. Why don't you come to New York? You can hear me play in a gig when I get one. My band broke up, but who needs them? I can make it on my own."

Izzy slurred and staggered more and more as the afternoon turned to evening. By the time people were telling Emma that they'd had a wonderful time and saying to Claire that they wished Richard and her the happiest life in Sydney together, Izzy was struggling to breathe in the bathroom.

Izzy had managed to gag and heave the vomit out of her airway before collapsing onto the bathroom floor next to the toilet. Tarryn had found her lying there when she'd visited the bathroom for herself.

Everyone remaining in the cottage had looked at each other as though they had survived an apocalypse. Roscoe and Thurston had held their arms around their wives' shoulders, as though to protect them from exposure to more trauma. They had approached Sam and whispered to him that they'd better head back to the brewery without him. He'd nodded, and they'd said a quiet goodnight. Luke had stayed with his father; he knew Songbird Cottage was where he was meant to be.

The only people left at the cottage were close family. Emma felt she was finally able to voice her opinion. "All right, what are we going to do about all this?"

Everyone knew Emma was not referring to cleaning up the party debris or the scandal Izzy had created for them; they all knew she was referring to helping Izzy.

"She's going to spend the rest of her life in a rehab facility, *that's* what's going to happen," John expostulated his opinion to the room, his face red with anger.

Sam nodded at Luke, and his son took a hesitant step forward. He stared around the room at all the outraged faces: Claire looked annoyed, Richard looked resigned, Emma was in shock, and John was chugging down a bottle of water as though he was determined to flush the three glasses of champagne he'd drunk over the course of the afternoon right out of his system.

"I was an addict, and I think I know how to help," Luke said quietly.

"What's that? What's that you said?" John put down his bottle and looked over at Luke.

"I can help Izzy. I know what she's going through and what steps we can take."

Emma turned sideways and replied to Luke's statement kindly, "You mean the twelve-step program, Luke?"

Luke moved into the middle of the room where everyone could see and hear him clearly, "No, I don't mean that. I saw Izzy before I came here. I've seen how she's been living, and it all feeds into her current behavior."

"And how would that be exactly, seeing as you're apparently the expert," John said from his perch on the sofa.

Luke described the sight that had met him when he'd arrived at Izzy's high-end apartment in Manhattan. The building was inhabited by young successful professionals—and this, Luke claimed, was part of the problem.

"What! There's no way that apartment is part of the problem! Izzy asked me to buy that place for her when she turned twenty-five. She said it was perfect for her." John was irate.

"You misunderstand me, John," Luke said calmly, "Izz might have thought that apartment was ideal for her four years ago, back when she had dreams of making it big in a rock band, but how do you think it makes her feel now? She's surrounded by successful individuals who have somewhere to go and something to do every day, while she's living in the same building as they are, except with no band and no job. It's a vicious cycle."

Everyone in the room stayed silent this time and politely waited to hear what Luke had to say next.

Luke went on to tell them that Izzy's apartment was a basic shell. Many of the fixtures and fittings had been ripped out of the walls and ceilings; the only appliance left in the kitchen was a kettle and that had a telltale shortened electrical cord. Luke explained that addicts used the copper from appliance cords to supply them with the copper tamping they needed for their pipes.

"To be honest with you, this would have been pretty darn obvious to anyone who had bothered to visit her," Luke stated emphatically.

More silence in the room.

Luke continued, "Addiction is more of an adaptation to your environment and your circumstances. If you are surrounded by stimulating company and have work to do, you don't need to go looking for fake stimulation to block out the drudgery or horror of your life."

"Tell them about Izzy's relationship," Sam interjected.

"Oh, well, Izzy had hooked up with an archetypal upwardly mobile professional guy in her building. She had considered them an item, and I'm sure to Izz that it must have had all the appearances of a relationship. But it wasn't. He had met her in the lobby of their building and had presumed she was on the same career trajectory as he was. By the time they started dating, he realized that Izzy wasn't suitable wife, or even girlfriend material, in his opinion, but he kept stringing her along with late night sleepovers and the occasional takeout and beer night. It suited him— he got to have a convenient warm body for pleasure and pizza, I guess. When he found someone he preferred more, I presume someone who was employed nine to five like he was, he dumped Izzy. Told her she was crazy to think he would be with a loser like her. She told me this on the drive up here."

"We're guessing that's when her social drinking and drug consumption blew up," Sam said.

John shifted uncomfortably on the sofa. "Seems a bit weak-willed to me," he huffed.

Ignoring John, Luke explained that Izzy had been trying to buy friendship and companionship ever since. She would contact all the lowlifes she'd gotten to know at her downtown gigs when she had played in the band and invite them over with the lure of as much free drugs and alcohol as they liked. She had promised Luke that she had never participated in that much drug using, but she hadn't been able to stop herself from telling him the rest of her story. It was as though she were bursting with the need to share her misery with someone.

"She's even mortgaged the apartment to pay for that toxic lifestyle. Every day she'd wake up and tell herself it was the end, that she'd never do it again. Then the loneliness and depression would kick in, and she'd be on the phone again the next evening, calling all those scroungers to come around and party with her again or going out to a bar to find more of them."

Emma stood from her chair at the dining table. "Okay, thanks

Luke, I've heard enough. Now, what do we plan to do about this?'

John opened his mouth to say "rehab" again, but Claire poked him hard in the ribs with her finger.

Luke sighed and shared, "I tore myself away from all the bad influences in my life. I went to work on the sheep farm. There's nothing out there except sky, earth, and animals. It cleared my head and allowed me to detox naturally."

"That might be all very well for you," John said, keeping one eye on Claire to see if she planned on poking him again, "but I'm not sending my daughter all the way to South Africa to sit on some desert farm surrounded by livestock."

"Nope, I'm not suggesting that," Luke replied, "but Izzy does need some kind of geographical rehabilitation. So, I want to take her on a hiking trip around Cabot Trail. She hasn't been doing this long enough for her to have built up a physiological dependence on alcohol and drugs, and it's just what she needs to get her away from Manhattan and her bad news 'friends.' What do you all think?"

Everyone in the room looked at each other. There was hope dawning on their faces and relief showing in everyone's eyes.

"That's settled then. Where can I find the nearest hiking goods store tomorrow?" Luke asked with a smile.

Chapter Seven: The Trail

"We're going to start our hike at the Acadian trail and camp at Chéticamp," Luke said to Claire as she came out of Izzy's bedroom.

"Uh-uh," Claire replied, softly closing the door behind her, "I'm ashamed to say I haven't been hiking for a long while. It's seems such a crime when I'm surrounded by all of God's majestic scenic grandeur."

Luke had two backpacks on the dining table, and he was busy stuffing each one with supplies.

"Luke," Claire came closer, and whispered, "How come she's not going through withdrawal? I've been looking for signs and symptoms, but Izzy seems fine. It's only embarrassment that's preventing her from coming out of the room."

Luke stopped packing to answer Claire, "Cocaine and crack are psychologically addictive and not a chemical dependency. Once you've crashed down off them, the only craving comes from your mind, not your body. Izzy's an alcoholic, first and foremost, and she used the cocaine to enable her to drink more, that's all. Unfortunately, cocaine loses its effectiveness quite soon during a binge session, so when alcoholics can't get any higher from the coke, they often turn to crack."

Claire grimaced, "Eeesh! I'd rather face reality than go through all that trouble."

"That's what every non-addict says," Luke said and went back to packing.

Sam and Emma came in from the garden. There was still some cleaning and clearing away from the party that had to be done. All the tableware had been washed, rinsed, dried, and packed back into the crates, waiting to be taken back to the brewery.

"Remind me to buy a dishwasher for Songbird Cottage before throwing another shindig here," Emma said as she sat down heavily on the velvet sofa.

"What's the point, Mom?" Claire said, "After Richard and I leave, no one's going to be staying here anymore."

Emma slapped her forehead with her hand, "Of course! I keep forgetting! It's become a habit to think of someone living at Songbird Cottage. Maybe your Dad could stay here…."

"I doubt it, Mom. Dad loves his high-tech boats and RVs too much to stay here."

Everyone turned at the sound of Izzy's voice. She had come quietly into the living area fully dressed, wearing hiking boots, jeans, and a flannel shirt. She turned to Luke and asked, "Finished packing, partner?"

"Yah," Luke replied, "We should get to Chéticamp in about forty-five minutes if we leave now."

Izzy turned to face her family after shrugging into her backpack and allowing Luke to adjust the straps for her. "Well, this is it, guys. Don't bother Dad and Richard; I prefer to sneak away while they're busy." She walked to where Emma and Sam stood. "Goodbye Mom, Sam. Once again, I'm sorry for ruining your party." Then she went to hug Claire, "Bye, big sis. Sorry to you, too."

Luke and Izzy walked out to the rental, threw their packs into the trunk, and drove off down the road. Neither of them looked back.

∞ ∞ ∞

Later that day, Luke and Izzy found themselves overlooking the Chéticamp River with a panoramic view of the Acadian coastline stretching out before them on either side. Luke had planned ahead for them to stop at the Parks Canada Visitor Center at the pretty fishing village of Chéticamp and pick up a park pass and trail location map. He had also planned a little surprise for Izzy.

There was a man waiting for them outside the visitors' center. He handed Luke a small basket covered with a blanket. The contents of the basket gave a yelp from under the blanket. Izzy pulled back the cover and saw a young terrier crossbreed trying to climb out.

"Wait!" Luke laughed, "don't let him get down until you have hold of his leash."

Izzy fussed and cuddled the little dog while Luke thanked the man who had brought him.

"What is this doggy for, Luke?" Izzy asked, keeping a firm hold of the dog's extendable leash while the excited hound ran sniffing around the lawn.

"He's a rescue dog from the mainland. We don't have enough incidences of animal cruelty on the island for me to have found a companion for our hike here, so that kind gentleman brought him to Cape Breton from Halifax. Doggo's so excited because he spent the first two years of his life on a chain in someone's backyard. Here, put these booties on him so his paws don't get sore. This is going to be his first hike."

The hike had gone smoothly after that. The Cape Breton weather was ideal for hiking at that time in May. The spring flowers hadn't faded from the summer heat yet. Trees were covered in a riot of freshly unfurled leaves, and when they drooped over the blooms and ferns, all the colors of the rainbow could be seen around them as they turned their heads from side to side.

Izzy inhaled the intoxicating odors of upturned soil, dew-dampened foliage, and river-rounded pebbles. She didn't feel like smoking at all. It was far nicer to smell what nature had to offer. After a while, her backpack stopped feeling like a burden, and instead, she felt her stomach rumble in anticipation of what food would be inside. All around her, she discovered new sights and sounds: the scamper of small animals in the bushes, the cry of large birds of prey and seagulls in the sky above. The terrier crossbreed took full advantage of his extendable leash and scurried from side to side, sniffing and sneezing at interesting things along the trail.

Izzy and Luke took a break at the trail's northernmost viewpoint. They sat on the grass and leaned back against their packs. Just as tired as them, the little terrier plopped down beside them after having a drink of water from a bowl Luke took out of his pack pocket. L'Acadien Trail stretched in a great arching loop on either side from where they sat. They could see where the river joined the ocean, its banks sweeping in a green embrace around the blue seacoast curves.

Izzy sighed and tilted her head back so that her face could bask in the late afternoon sun.

"I'd forgotten how beautiful the Gulf of St. Lawrence is," she said to Luke in a contented voice. "I remember how Claire and I would stand and stare at those rippling waves for hours when we were children, hoping to spot a whale."

"And did you?" Luke asked as he threaded the dog's ears gently around his fingers.

"I remember we saw a whale on one of our visits up here, but to be honest, I can't remember which coastline it was from. Funny the things you think you'll never ever forget when you're a child, are often some of the first memories to fade away into a mist." Izzy gave another deep sigh.

"The pineal gland gets messed up from cocaine," Luke said, "that's why addicts struggle to sleep and remember certain things. And childhood amnesia is caused by memories over-loading the hippocampus, which isn't developed enough in young children to be able to store the experience as a long-term memory."

Izzy turned to Luke, "Gosh, Luke, I didn't realize you were such a—fountain of knowledge."

"Ha!" Luke threw back his head and laughed, "you were going to say, 'fountain of useless information,' weren't you!"

Izzy joined him in laughing, and they continued chuckling and chatting all the way back down the trail until they reached the campground.

"Which trail do you want to do tomorrow, Izz?" Luke asked that evening. "We can go anywhere except the Skyline Trail—too many moose, so dogs aren't allowed."

Izzy looked at her map. "Well, seeing as we're here, we may as well do Salmon Falls next and then hop along from Le Chemin du Buttereau all the way up to Corney Brook. Then we can skip Skyline, and head back inland towards Bog and Benjie's Lake. How does that sound?"

Luke was busy stirring hot water over their noodles. He nodded. "Sounds like a plan, Izz." He went back to stirring the pot. After sprinkling over the seasoning and checking that every dehydrated vegetable had been well soaked, he poured half the noodles into a rectangular tin bowl and handed it to Izzy.

"I wonder how Benjie's Lake got its name?" Izzy mused between taking loud slurps of noodles.

"I have no idea," Luke confessed, "probably named for some long-forgotten sheepherder or his dog."

Izzy looked over at the small terrier who lay fast asleep next to where they sat. "I think we should call him Benjy."

"He's your dog, Izz," Luke replied, "you can call him whatever you like."

Izzy stopped eating, with her foldout fork halfway between her mouth and her bowl, "*My* dog? But my building is strictly no pets allowed! I won't be able to keep him—Benjy—when I go back."

"Then don't go back." Luke regarded Izzy with a steady gaze. "Don't go back to that depressing apartment, Izz. Why would you even want to?"

Luke bent down, picked up the dozing Benjy, and placed him gently on his lap. He held the small dog's paw in his hand and put on a high-pitched, squeaky voice, "Don't go back to Manhattan, Mommy Izzy, please. Stay here in Pleasant Bay and take me for walks every day." With every word, Luke waved the dog's paw as though emphasizing the point he was trying to make.

Izzy couldn't help it. She burst out laughing so hard that she nearly fell off the foldout chair on which she was sitting. After a while, she grew quiet again, a small frown on her face. "I'm not a coward, Luke, I'm not going to retreat from Manhattan like a coward. After all, living there is the only thing I've got going for me. And I don't like the thought of everyone I know there saying I couldn't hack it."

Luke listened to what she had to say and nodded in understanding. Izzy realized the act of having someone listen, truly listen, to her words and thoughts, was something she hadn't experienced for a long time. For the last four years of her life, Izzy had either said things she thought other people wanted to hear, or she had been surrounded by people who were only waiting for her to finish speaking so that they could talk themselves. This realization swept over Izzy like a strong sea breeze.

Luke watched Izzy carefully. He knew his future lay with Isabelle Havisham—had known it since they had been very small children, playing together during every school vacation. They had gone separate ways as teenagers. The stressful life in South Africa had darkened Luke's outlook and heightened his naturally thoughtful temperament until it had turned into a deep depression. It had started when his mom and Sam had bought him a scooter for his sixteenth birthday. He'd pulled up at a red traffic light in Cape Town one evening and been held up at gunpoint by two young men. They had pulled him off the scooter and ridden off with it, but not until they had beaten him so badly that his mother and father had feared for his life.

Teenaged Luke had tried climbing his way out of depression with the use of drugs. But it had been his online chats with Izzy that had made him realize he had to change or die. Like all part-time habitual drug users, Izzy had been great at helping Luke face his demons. He'd recovered just in time to be able to help her in return.

The young couple stared at each other across the wooden decking that was still warm from the setting sun. A world of possibility was visible to Isabelle in her mind. Leave New York, leave seeking elusive fame as a rock musician, leave her fake friends, leave heartache. Leave it all behind.

"What are you thinking?" Luke asked. "I've tried, but I can't read your mind."

"Leave…leaving," Izzy murmured.

Fear jolted Luke, "You want to leave? Please don't leave, Izzy! I've loved you since I was a boy. We were friends, and…and, it just turned to love naturally over time. You deserve to be loved so much."

Benjy picked up on Luke's sadness and gave a loud bark.

Izzy stood up, "You are the cutest dog I have ever known, Benjy, and as for your master…."

Izzy walked over to where Luke sat with the wriggling Benjy on his lap. She bent over and kissed Luke on the top of his head. Then she knelt down beside his chair and kissed him long and lovingly, full on the lips. Luke allowed Benjy to jump out of his arms, so he could wrap both around Izzy and pull her closer. They stayed like that for many minutes. The weight of sadness and loneliness within them became lighter with every passing second.

"I love you too, Luke," Izzy said huskily when they finally broke apart, "I want to stay with you at Songbird Cottage in Pleasant Bay, forever."

"Then that's what we'll do, my darling Isabelle, that's what we'll do."

<h1 style="text-align:center">Epilogue</h1>

Songbird Cottage was hardly recognizable as the old summer vacation home slash converted barn it had once been. Isabelle and Luke had spent the summer painting over flaking red paint on the walls outside and adding on an extension.

Sam was there to oversee their handiwork, and Richard would pop by on weekends to help them with construction.

"We're going to need a bigger barn," Luke joked with his family.

The news that Richard and Claire were expecting their first child had sent Sam and Luke running for blueprints to figure out the best way to add another guestroom and bathroom onto the cottage.

"Are you sure we only need to make space for one baby?" Isabelle would tease her brother-in-law by saying, "Maybe that ex-girlfriend of yours' baby turns out to be yours after all!"

"You're lucky I'm not able to swing this plank around and smack you with it, Isabelle!" Richard joked. "The paternity tests proved irrevocably that she was talking nonsense."

Claire and Emma came out to the busy builders, holding two trays full of lemonade in plastic cups.

"Don't mention that horrible woman to us ever again!" Claire said, but the smile on her face took the edge off her words. "Dad called to say he's on his way in the RV, by the way, and he's bringing Kate with him."

Sam added his thoughts to the conversation, "Maybe we should make the extension a bit bigger? In case your father wants his own bedroom in the cottage for him and Kate?"

Claire, Emma, and Isabelle shouted out together in a chorus, "You can't separate John from his beloved high-tech stuff!" and they all laughed together, with Claire saying, "Jinx, you owe me a drink!"

Everyone dropped their tools and gathered under the shade of the tallest red maple to have their mid-morning break. As they sat there, a brilliantly deep scarlet leaf fluttered to the ground.

"Fall's on its way," Luke said somberly, as he stroked Benjy's fur.

"Yes, another season has come and gone in Pleasant Bay," Emma said wistfully. "Who knows what the next year will bring for the Havishams, MacAuleys, and Bensons?"

Richard reached over to pat his wife's tummy lovingly, "Well, Emma, for sure it's going to bring us a baby!"

Claire grabbed his hand and held it against the side of her waist. "She's kicking again, can you feel that?"

"I want to feel, too!" Isabelle went to sit with her sister and gently laid a hand on Claire's baby bump.

"Why do you sound sad when you say fall's coming, love?" Isabelle asked Luke as she sat beside her sister. "You aren't thinking about avoiding winter and heading on back to South Africa, are you?"

In true South African style, Luke had enjoyed joking about how temperate the climate was back in his old country. It was something every South African did after they moved to North America.

Luke laughed, "In all honesty, the Karoo winters in South Africa are just as cold as the ones here on Cape Breton! And the summers are brutally hot, so there's no way I'm ever heading back to that place! What made me sad was this—I thought about how we are so lucky and blessed if we get to experience more than seventy-five summers in one lifetime, you know? That's such a low number, if you think about it."

There was silence as everyone digested what Luke had said. Only a limited number of buckets hanging from the maple trees in spring, or honey collected from the beehives, summer visits to the beach, leaves falling to the ground, and warm winter fires to snuggle beside.

Isabelle broke the silence, "It's only at Pleasant Bay where I'm able to feel the richness of my life. When I lived in Manhattan, I wasn't aware of the passage of time. It was just a blur of mornings and evenings blending into one. I could see the trees lose their leaves and the sun rising and setting, but I couldn't feel it."

"It must be scary to wake up one day and realize your life could have been better if you'd only taken the time to reconnect with the seasons and the sun," Sam said thoughtfully.

Claire, Emma, and Isabelle looked at each other after Sam said this. It was as if their minds were bonded together and they were able to read each other's thoughts.

Yes, we each nearly became one of those people—someone who allows her life to slip by uncelebrated and unacknowledged. How did it happen that we lived so many years in a fog of unhappiness without even knowing it? It was only when we came to live at Songbird Cottage that we could begin to live and love forever.

Thank you, readers!

Thank you for reading this book. It is important to me to share my stories with you and that you enjoy them. May I ask of you a favor? If you enjoyed this book, will you please take a moment to leave a review on Amazon and/or Goodreads? Thank you for your support!

Also, each week, I send my readers updates about my life as well as information about my new releases, freebies, promos, and book recommendations. If you're interested in receiving my weekly newsletter, please go to newsletter.sylviaprice.com, and it will ask you for your email. As a thank-you, you will receive a FREE exclusive short story that isn't available for purchase!

Blessings,
Sylvia

Books In This Series

Pleasant Bay

Songbird Cottage Beginnings

Get it for FREE!

Sam MacAuley and his wife Annalize are total opposites. When Sam wants to leave city life in Halifax to get a plot of land on Cape Breton Island, where he grew up, his wife wants nothing to do with his plans and opts to move herself and their three boys back to her home country of South Africa.

As Sam settles into a new life on his own, his friend Lachlan encourages him to get back into the dating scene. Although he meets plenty of women, he longs to find the one with whom he wants to share the rest of his life. Will Sam ever meet "the one"?

to resent him, she chooses, instead, to find him. Her misfortunes pile up in her quest to return Jonah to the Amish faith, but she is undeterred, for God has given her a mission.

Will Mary Lou's faith be enough to help them get through the countless obstacles that are thrown their way? Do Jonah and Mary Lou have a chance at happiness?

Join Jonah and Mary Lou as they wrestle with love, a life worth living, and their unique faith in Christ. Enjoy the conclusion of Jonah's Redemption in this exclusive boxed set, with a bonus epilogue and companion story!

The Christmas Arrival: An Amish Holiday Romance

Rachel Lapp is a young Amish woman who is the daughter of the community's bishop. She is in the midst of planning the annual Christmas Nativity play when newcomer Noah Miller arrives in town to spend Christmas with his cousins. Encouraged by her father to welcome the new arrival, Rachel asks Noah to be a part of the Nativity.

Despite Rachel's engagement to Samuel King, a local farmer, she finds herself irrevocably drawn to Noah and his carefree spirit. Reserved and slightly shy, Noah is hesitant to get involved in the play, but an unlikely friendship begins to develop between Rachel and Noah, bringing with it unexpected problems, including a seemingly harmless prank with life-threatening consequences that require a Christmas miracle.

Will Rachel honor her commitment to Samuel, or will Noah win her affections?

Join these characters on what is sure to be a heartwarming holiday adventure! Instead of waiting for each part to be released, enjoy the entire Christmas Arrival series in this exclusive collection!

About the Author

Sylvia Price

Now an Amazon bestselling author, Sylvia Price is an author of Amish and contemporary romance and women's fiction. She especially loves writing uplifting stories about second chances!

Although raised in the cosmopolitan city of Montréal, Sylvia spent her adolescent and young adult years in Nova Scotia, and the beautiful countryside landscapes and ocean views serve as the backdrop to her contemporary novels.

After meeting and falling in love with an American while living abroad, Sylvia now resides in the US. She spends her days writing, hoping to inspire the next generation to read more stories. When she's not writing, Sylvia stays busy making sure her three young children are alive and well-fed.

Subscribe to Sylvia's newsletter at newsletter.sylviaprice.com to stay in the loop about new releases, freebies, promos, and more. As a thank-you, you will receive a FREE exclusive short story that isn't available for purchase.

Learn more about Sylvia at amazon.com/author/sylviaprice and goodreads.com/author/show/1134593.Sylvia_Price.

Follow Sylvia on Facebook at facebook.com/sylviapriceauthor for updates.

Join Sylvia's Advanced Reader Copies (ARC) team at arcteam.sylviaprice.com to get her books for free before they are released in exchange for honest reviews.